1764
MEET
KAYA

An American Girl

BY JANET SHAW

ILLUSTRATIONS BILL FARNSWORTH

VIGNETTES SUSAN MCALILEY

Published by Pleasant Company Publications
Copyright © 2002 by Pleasant Company
All rights reserved. No part of this book may be used or reproduced
in any manner whatsoever without written permission except in the
case of brief quotations embodied in critical articles and reviews.
For information, address: Book Editor, Pleasant Company Publications,
8400 Fairway Place, P.O. Box 620998, Middleton, WI 53562.

Visit our Web site at **americangirl.com**

Printed in China.
02 03 04 05 06 07 08 LEO 12 11 10 9 8 7 6 5 4 3 2

The American Girls Collection®, Kaya™, and American Girl®
are trademarks of Pleasant Company.

PICTURE CREDITS
The following individuals and organizations have generously given
permission to reprint images contained in "Looking Back":

pp. 62–63—© W. Perry Conway/CORBIS (IH 191598) (coyote); Reproduced with kind
permission from the Eelahweemah (David Williams) family, The Chief Joseph Band of Nez Perce
on the Colville Reservation, photo courtesy of MSCUA, University of Washington Libraries,
Neg. NA986 (women and children); pp. 64–65—Photo courtesy of National Park Service, Nez Perce
National Historical Park (NEPE-1786) (spearing salmon); *Inland Fishes of Washington*, by
R.S. Wydoski and R.R. Whitney (sockeye salmon); Oregon Historical Society (OrHi 4466) (mat lodge);
pp. 66–67—Fourth of July Celebration photograph from the Chief Joseph Band of Nez Perce on
the Colville Reservation, photo courtesy of National Park Service, Nez Perce National Historical
Park (NEPE-2279) (women riding); Photo by Chuck Williams (Appaloosa); Photo courtesy of
National Park Service, Nez Perce National Historical Park (NEPE-1773) (Lewis and Clark);
pp. 68–69—Missouri Historical Society, St. Louis (Lewis and Clark journal); Idaho State Historical
Society, photo by E. Jane Gay (63-221.83/b) (reservation); Russell Lamb Photography, Portland, OR
(football); Ben Marra, www.benmarra.com, Lolita, Nez Perce/Colville (modern girl dancer).

Library of Congress Cataloging-in-Publication Data

Shaw, Janet Beeler, 1937–
Meet Kaya : an American girl / by Janet Shaw ;
illustrations, Bill Farnsworth ; vignettes, Susan McAliley.

p. cm. — (The American girls collection)
Summary: In 1764, when Kaya and her family reunite with other Nez Perce Indians
to fish for the red salmon, she learns that bragging, even about her swift horse,
can lead to trouble. Includes historical notes on the Nez Perce Indians.
ISBN 1-58485-424-3 — ISBN 1-58485-423-5 (pbk.)
[1. Pride and vanity—Fiction. 2. Conduct of life—Fiction. 3. Horses—Fiction.
4. Nez Perce Indians—Fiction. 5. Indians of North America—Northwest, Pacific—Fiction.
6. Northwest, Pacific—Fiction.] I. Farnsworth, Bill, ill. II. McAliley, Susan, ill. III. Title.
PZ7.S53423 Me 2002 [Fic]—dc21 2001036810

TO THE NEZ PERCE
GIRLS AND BOYS,
MOTHERS AND FATHERS,
GRANDMOTHERS AND GRANDFATHERS,
UNTO THE SEVENTH GENERATION

Kaya and her family are *Nimíipuu*, known today as Nez Perce Indians. They speak the Nez Perce language, so you'll see some Nez Perce words in this book. "Kaya" is short for the Nez Perce name *Kaya'aton'my'*, which means "she who arranges rocks." You'll find the meanings and pronunciations of these and other Nez Perce words in the glossary on page 70.

TABLE OF CONTENTS

KAYA'S FAMILY

TOE-TA
Kaya's father, an expert horseman and wise village leader.

EETSA
Kaya's mother, who is a good provider for her family and her village.

KAYA
An adventurous girl with a generous spirit.

BROWN DEER
Kaya's sister, who is old enough to court.

WING FEATHER AND SPARROW
Kaya's mischievous twin brothers.

KALUTSA
AND AALAH
*Toe-ta's parents,
who teach Kaya
the old ways.*

SPEAKING RAIN
*A blind girl who lives
with Kaya's family and
is a sister to her.*

STEPS HIGH
Kaya's beloved horse.

RAVEN
*A boy who loves to
race horses.*

FOX TAIL
*A bothersome boy
who can be rude.*

CHAPTER
ONE
—

LET'S RACE!

 When Kaya and her family rode over the hill into *Wallowa*, The Valley of the Winding Waters, her horse pricked up her ears and whinnied. Answering whinnies came from the large herd grazing nearby. Kaya stroked the smooth shoulder of her horse.

"Go easy, Steps High," she said softly. "We'll be there soon." But Steps High whinnied again and began to prance, stepping high just like her name. Speaking Rain's old pony whinnied, too. A sickness in Speaking Rain's eyes had caused her to lose her sight, so Kaya held the lead rope of her pony.

"I hear so many horses!" Speaking Rain said. "What do you see, Kaya? Tell me." Because

1

Speaking Rain's parents had died, she'd lived
with Kaya's family and was a sister to her.

Kaya studied the white-peaked mountains,
the broad valley, and the shining lake
so she could share the beauty of this
beloved place with her blind sister.

"The snow's still deep on the
mountains," Kaya said. "The lake reflects
the green hills and the blue sky. The river's full of
red salmon and running higher than I've ever
seen it. The tepees are set far back from the bank."

"Where is everyone?" Speaking Rain
asked. She held her buckskin doll against
her chest.

"Some men are spearfishing in the river,"
Kaya said. "Some little boys are tossing up a hoop
and trying to shoot arrows through it. Little girls
are playing near the tepees, and all along the shore
women are cleaning and drying salmon."

"I've smelled the salmon for a long time,"
Speaking Rain said. "It's a powerful scent! The
men must have a big catch this year."

It was midsummer, the season when the salmon
swam upstream to the lake to lay their eggs. Many

bands of *Nimíipuu* gathered here each year to catch
and dry the salmon. Kaya and her family were
traveling with several other families from Salmon
River Country to join the fishing. Her family was
also visiting her father's parents. Kaya loved these
reunions with her grandparents and her many other
relatives, old and young—all the children were just
like brothers and sisters to each other.

Kaya's mother and her older sister, Brown Deer,
rode just ahead. Her mother glanced back over her
shoulder, then reined in her horse and motioned for
Brown Deer and Kaya to do the same.

"What is it, *Eetsa?*" Kaya asked her mother.

"The bundles on my pack horse have slipped a
little. They'll rub a sore spot if I don't balance them
again," Eetsa said. "I need to retie them."

Eetsa and Brown Deer quickly slipped off their
horses and began untying some woven bags from
a pack horse. Wing Feather, one of Kaya's twin
brothers, had been riding behind Eetsa's saddle.
The other twin, Sparrow, rode behind Brown Deer's.
It had been a long journey, and the little boys
were restless. Kaya helped the twins down so they
could stretch their legs. The boys giggled as they

scampered to hide behind a travois and
peeked over, their dark eyes gleaming.

"Look after your brothers well,"
Eetsa told Kaya, as she always did. Eetsa

travois

and Brown Deer hung several woven bags of dried
roots and dried buffalo meat on their saddle horns.

As they worked, they glanced eagerly at the
tepees along the river. Kaya smiled to herself. She
was thinking that Nimíipuu loved to travel, but they
loved the excitement of arrival even more. Already
her grandfather and two of her uncles were riding
out to greet them.

"I'm so glad we're here!" Brown Deer said.
She smoothed her buckskin dress and touched the
abalone shells she wore in her ears. "Remember
what fun we had the last time we visited?"

Kaya nodded. *"Aa-heh!* I remember
what fun you had dancing every night!
I wonder which boys will serenade you
this time," she teased. After the hard work came
hours of trading and games. There would be feasting,
singing, and always dancing, with the beat of the
drums echoing down the valley.

Kaya turned and saw her father gazing at the

herd of sleek horses, some of them spotted, in the wide meadow. Perhaps *Toe-ta* was thinking of trading for some of the horses, or of the races they'd have. He was an expert horseman. Often he won races on his fleet-footed stallion.

Kaya was certainly thinking about horse races. For a long time she'd imagined being in one on her adored Steps High. She knew Steps High was fast, but also young and untested. Toe-ta had told her that Steps High wasn't ready to race yet.

When Eetsa was satisfied that everything was in order, she and Brown Deer mounted their horses. Kaya helped the little boys climb back onto the patient animals and take their places again.

When Kaya turned to Steps High, the horse tossed her head and pawed the ground. Kaya rubbed her cheek against Steps High's soft muzzle. "If only we could race I know we'd win!" she whispered as she climbed into the saddle.

"Did you say something to me?" Speaking Rain asked, as Kaya took her pony's lead rope again.

"I was talking to Steps High," Kaya said. "I told her that when we race we'll beat all the others!"

Eetsa turned to look Kaya in the eye. "I've told

you before not to boast," she said firmly. "Our actions speak for us. Our deeds show our worth. Let that be your lesson, Kaya."

Kaya pressed her lips together—she knew Eetsa was right.

"Come, let's meet the others," Toe-ta said, and led the way on his stallion.

⟁

When Kaya and her family rode up, her grandmother, *Aalah*, and one of her aunts were waiting at the doorway of their tepee. Aalah stepped forward. Her face was creased with age, and little pockmarks, like fingerprints, covered her cheeks.

"*Tawts may-we!*" she said. "Welcome, my son! Welcome, all of you!" Smiling, she hugged Kaya and Speaking Rain as soon as they climbed off their horses. Then she took the twins into her arms. She kissed their chubby cheeks and tugged their braids.

"Tawts may-we!" Eetsa said. As Toe-ta and the others dismounted and shared greetings, she took the woven bags from her saddle horn. "We brought these for you," she said, offering their gifts with pleasure—it was an honor to give them.

6

Aalah received the gifts with thanks. Then
Auntie put one hand on Kaya's shoulder and her
other hand on Speaking Rain's. "You've grown! Are
you hard workers like your sister, Brown Deer?"

"Aa-heh! We are!" Kaya and Speaking Rain said
at the same time, and giggled.

"*Tawts!*" Auntie nodded. "You girls help Brown
Deer unpack the horses and bring your things inside."

Kaya and Brown Deer carried their bundles
into the tepee and placed them across from where
their grandparents slept. Speaking Rain stacked the
bundles neatly along the wall of the tepee. It was

always packed full when they gathered here. But Kaya liked it crowded and cozy, and the tule mats that covered the tepee let in cool breezes and light.

tule mats

After the women and girls had put everything in order around the tepee, Eetsa allowed Kaya to take Speaking Rain and the little boys to play. "Remember, it's your job to look after your brothers carefully," she reminded Kaya.

Kaya knew there were dangerous animals about. She also knew about the Stick People—small, mischievous people who might lure a child to wander too far away into the woods. "Aa-heh," Kaya said. "I will."

She led Speaking Rain and the twins to a group of boys and girls gathered in the shade beside the river. Raven, a boy a little older than Kaya, was playing a game with a length of hemp cord.

"Here's what happened when Coyote went to put up his tepee," Raven said. The twins watched, wide-eyed, as Raven's fingers flashed, weaving the cord into the shape of a tepee. Then, with a tug, he made the tepee collapse. "Coyote worked too fast!"

he said. "He didn't tie the poles properly, and his tepee fell down on him!" Everyone laughed and the twins squealed at the fun.

Raven leaned back on his elbows in the thick grass. "I see you have a new horse, Little Sister," he said to Kaya. "She's a pretty one."

"She's the prettiest horse in the whole herd!" Kaya said. She couldn't disguise her pride. Steps High wasn't large, only about thirteen hands high. She had a black head and chest, a white rump with black spots on it, and a white star on her forehead. "She's fast, too," Kaya added. *That wasn't boasting,* she thought—just saying what was true.

Fox Tail squatted beside her. He was a bothersome boy who could be rude. He always followed Raven, trying to impress the older boy. "Your horse looks skittish to me," he said to Kaya. "Why would your father give you a horse like that?"

"Toe-ta didn't choose my horse," Kaya said. "My horse chose me."

Fox Tail laughed and slapped his leg. "Your horse chose you? How?"

"One day I was riding by the herd with Toe-ta,"

Kaya said. "A filly kept nickering to me. So I whistled to her. She followed me. She came up to me and pushed her head against my leg. Toe-ta said that meant she wanted to be my horse. He worked with her so I could ride her."

"Is that a true story?" Fox Tail demanded.

"Ask my father if that's true," Kaya said.

"I believe you," Raven said. "But you say she's fast. Should I believe that, too?"

"I haven't raced her yet, but I've run her many times," Kaya said. "She glides over the ground like the shadow of an eagle."

Fox Tail jumped to his feet. "Like an eagle—big talk!" he said. "Let's race our horses and see if yours flies like you claim she does!"

"Yes, let's race!" Raven got to his feet, too.

Kaya had an uneasy feeling. *I shouldn't have boasted about her speed*, she thought. *I've never raced her.* "My horse is tired now," she said hesitantly.

"She's not too tired for one short race," Fox Tail insisted. "Maybe your horse isn't so fast, after all."

Kaya felt her face grow hot. Her horse was as swift as the wind! She was sired by Toe-ta's fine stallion, Runner.

Kaya stood up. "Speaking Rain, could you take care of the twins for me?" she asked. "I know it's my job, but I want to race."

Speaking Rain was braiding strands of grass into bracelets for the little boys. "I'll try, but sometimes they play tricks on me."

"I'll only be gone a little while," Kaya assured her.

Kaya, Raven, and Fox Tail got on their horses and rode up to the raised plain at the end of the lake. Often people held celebrations and races here on the level ground, but today Kaya and the boys were alone.

Now that she'd decided to race, Kaya was eager to begin. Steps High seemed eager, too. When Fox Tail's roan horse came close, Steps High arched her neck and flattened her ears. When Raven's chestnut horse passed her, she trotted faster.

Raven reined in his horse. "We'll start here. When I give the signal, we'll race until we pass that boulder at the far end of the field." He held his hand high. Then he brought it down and they were off!

The boys took the lead, stones spurting from under their horses' hooves. They lay low on their horses, their weight forward. They ran neck and neck.

Steps High bolted after them but swung out too

wide. Kaya pressed her heels into Steps High's sides. Then she gave Steps High her head, and her horse sprang forward.

Kaya thrilled to feel her horse gather herself, lengthen out, and gallop flat out! She was running as she'd never run before. Her long strides were so smooth that she seemed to be floating, her hooves barely touching the earth. Her dark mane whipped Kaya's face. Grit stung her lips. She clung to her horse, barely aware that they'd caught the other horses until they passed them. She and Steps High were in the lead!

Then, suddenly, Steps High began to buck! She plunged, head down, heels high. Kaya grasped her mane and hung on. She bit her tongue and tasted blood. Steps High bucked again!

Raven spun his horse around. He was beside Steps High in an instant and grabbed the rein. He pulled the horse sharply to him, and, in the same motion, he halted his own horse. Steps High skidded to a standstill, foam lathering her neck. Kaya slid off.

Steps High's eyes were wild. For a moment she seemed never to have been tamed at all. Kaya's legs were shaking badly, but her first thought was to

*Kaya clung to her horse, barely aware that they'd caught the other horses
until they passed them. She and Steps High were in the lead!*

calm her horse. She began to stroke Steps High's trembling head and neck.

Fox Tail came galloping back. "I knew that horse was skittish!" he cried. "She just proved it!"

"She proved she's fast, too," Raven said.

Kaya wanted to thank Raven for coming to her aid, but her wounded pride was a knife in her chest. She could hardly get her breath. Leading her horse slowly to cool her down, Kaya silently walked away from the boys.

When Kaya had rubbed down Steps High, she turned her horse out to graze. Then she started back through the woods, heading toward the river.

Her feelings were all tangled up like a nest of snakes. She was excited that Steps High had run so fast, but she was disappointed that her horse had broken her training. She was relieved that she hadn't been bucked off, but she wished the boys hadn't seen her lose control. She knew she shouldn't have boasted, but she also wished she could have made good on her boast and won the race.

When Kaya glanced up from nursing her hurt feelings, Fox Tail was coming down the trail toward her on foot. He stopped right in front of her. "You told us your horse chose you," he said with a smirk. "Would you choose her after the way she tried to buck you off today?"

"She's the best horse ever!" Kaya said. "She can run faster than your horse, and I can run faster than you, too. Want to race me right now?"

Fox Tail cocked his head. "The first one to the riverbank wins!" he cried. He turned and sprinted away down the path.

For a little while Kaya was right on his heels. Then Fox Tail left the path, leapt over a fallen log, and took off through the woods. *He must know a shortcut,* Kaya thought. She followed him.

But she couldn't keep him in sight because he jagged in and out of shadows. Was that his dark head beyond the bushes? Now she was uncertain which way to go. She stopped to listen for the sound of the river as her guide.

She stood in a gloomy clearing surrounded by black willows. She listened for rushing water. There was only silence. No wind blew in the leaves, no flies buzzed. All she could hear was her heartbeat.

Then a twig snapped behind her.

She whirled around. Did something just duck behind that tree? The shadows around her seemed to waver and sway. Was it the Stick People? Had they led her to this part of the woods?

Kaya held her breath. She knew the Stick People were cunning and crafty. They were strong, too. She'd heard they could carry off a baby and leave it a long way from its mother.

A flock of jays cawed—or was it the Stick People signaling to her? They seemed to be saying, "Forgot! Forgot!" Kaya shivered. What had she forgotten?

Then she gasped. She'd forgotten her little brothers! Kaya should never have given her job to Speaking Rain. The little boys were four winters old, just the right age for mischief. Kaya must get back to them at once, before they got into danger.

She knew she must leave a gift for the Stick People in return for their help. They became angry with people who didn't treat them respectfully. She found rose hips in the bag she wore on her belt and placed them on the moss. Then she began running back the way she'd come.

CHAPTER
TWO
—

SWITCHINGS!

 Kaya ran along the riverbank, past
women cleaning salmon and cutting the
fish into thin strips. Auntie was laying
the strips on racks to dry. She raised her hand in
greeting when Kaya rushed by.

But Kaya kept going. She ran up to some girls
setting up a little camp for their buckskin dolls.
They'd made a travois with sticks and pieces of an
old tule mat. A boy pretended to be their horse,
pulling the travois. "Have you seen Speaking Rain
and my brothers?" Kaya asked.

The children shook their heads, and Kaya ran
on, desperate to find them.

The twins had never been like other little boys.

They could understand each other without saying a word out loud. When they were born, the setting sun and the rising moon were both in the sky. Two lights in the sky and two babies who looked alike— they were special children. They could also be twice the trouble if they decided to play tricks.

Kaya ran through some brush and out onto the grassy bank where she'd last seen Speaking Rain with the boys. Speaking Rain crouched by a twisted pine tree, but the twins were nowhere in sight.

"Where are the boys?" Kaya called.

"I don't know," Speaking Rain said. "But I just found the toy I made for them." She held up a little hoop made of grass. "They got tired of my game and ran off. I've been calling them but they don't answer." Her cloudy eyes were wide with alarm. "Maybe they fell in the river!"

Kaya caught her breath. "Did you hear a splash?"

Speaking Rain shook her head. "But where could they be? Maybe a cougar chased them."

Cougars! Cougars sometimes went after small children. Kaya's heart raced, but she tried not to let Speaking Rain feel her alarm. "Come on, let's look for the boys. If they just ran off, they can't be far."

She made herself sound confident, but she was
frightened. The boys could be hurt or lost. Oh, why
hadn't she thought of them instead of herself?

Kaya looked around. Two trails led away from
the riverbank. One turned upstream
toward where the women worked.
The other turned downstream.
Dust-covered leaves hung low over
that trail. The little boys probably would have been
drawn to that leafy tunnel. "Boys!" Kaya called.
"Where are you?"

There was no answer.

"Follow me," Kaya said to Speaking Rain. "I'll
look and you listen."

Speaking Rain took hold of Kaya's sleeve and
walked right behind her down the trail.

"I see their footprints in the dust," Kaya said.
She walked faster. "And here's where they left the
trail and went under the bushes. They were
crawling. We'll have to crawl, too. Stay close."

The girls got down on their hands and knees
and inched forward. Leaves caught in their braids
and brushed their cheeks. Kaya kept a lookout for
the Stick People hiding in the shadows. Maybe

they'd led the boys deeper into the woods.

A little farther on, the prints disappeared. Kaya sat back on her heels. "I've lost their trail. Do you hear anything?"

Speaking Rain lifted her chin and frowned. "I hear the river. There's swift water there. If the boys fell in, they'd be swept away."

Kaya put her hand on Speaking Rain's shoulder. "Let's keep looking," she said. She began to search for prints again.

"I think we should get others to help us," Speaking Rain said. Then she pointed up. "Listen, I hear something up there!"

Kaya got to her feet so that she could see over the bushes. An old spruce tree loomed overhead. A cougar might be crouching in the branches! Or the boys. She'd been so busy following signs on the ground that she'd forgotten the twins could climb trees.

A spruce branch trembled. Two pairs of dark eyes gazed down at her from the green boughs. The boys were clinging to the trunk like raccoons. They were grinning.

Kaya was flooded with relief. She was also angry that the boys had scared her and Speaking Rain.

"Come down right now!" she said.

The little boys crept down out of the tree in a shower of dry needles. When they reached the ground, they started to giggle.

Kaya took their hands and crouched to look into their eyes. "Don't laugh!" she said. "Running off isn't a game. Dangers are everywhere!"

"Yes, dangers are everywhere," a low voice said.

Startled, Kaya and Speaking Rain turned. Someone was coming through the woods behind them.

Hands parted the branches, and Auntie stepped through. Her face was stern. "When you ran by me I sensed trouble, so I followed you," she said. "Now I see I was right. I heard your mother tell you to look after your brothers. But you ran away from your responsibility."

Kaya felt her face redden. She bit her lips. Auntie's words made her ache with shame. "I'm sorry," she whispered.

"You should be sorry," Auntie said in a weary voice. "I must call Whipwoman to teach you a lesson."

As Kaya followed Auntie back to the camp, she kept a strong hold on her feelings so that they wouldn't show, but her eyes stung with unshed tears.

She kept her gaze on her feet when Auntie went to fetch Whipwoman, the respected elder selected to discipline children who misbehaved.

When Whipwoman arrived, she carried a bundle of switches. But it wasn't the switches that Kaya dreaded—it was the bad opinion of the other children. When one child misbehaved, *all* the children were disciplined. They learned that what one of them did affected all the rest.

"Come here, children!" Whipwoman called out. "Come here now!"

One by one, the children old enough to be switched came forward and lined up in front of Whipwoman. She laid her bundle of willow switches on the ground at her feet.

"Lie down on your stomachs and bare your legs," Whipwoman told them. She waited while everyone did as she said.

Kaya lay down, pulled her skirt up to her knees, and pressed her mouth to the back of her hand. She heard the switch hiss through the air and felt it sting her bare legs. She winced, but she didn't cry out or make a sound. Whipwoman moved on to Speaking Rain, then to the next child. On and on she went

Kaya heard the switch hiss through the air and felt it sting her bare legs.
She winced, but she didn't cry out or make a sound.

23

until they'd all been given a switching.

As the children lay there, Whipwoman spoke to them slowly and firmly. "Kaya didn't watch out for her brothers. They ran off into the woods. They could have been injured. Enemies could have carried them away. A magpie that thinks only of itself would have given the boys better care than Kaya did! Nimíipuu always look out for each other. Our lives depend on it. Don't ever forget that, children. Now get up."

magpie

When Kaya lifted her head she caught sight of her parents and grandparents looking on. Their sad faces hurt her much more than the stings on her legs.

Fox Tail got to his knees near Kaya. He grimaced as he rubbed his legs. "Magpie!" he whispered to her. "I'm going to call you Magpie."

"Magpie! Magpie!" echoed the girl next to him.

Speaking Rain inched closer to Kaya and clasped her hand. "Don't mind them," Speaking Rain said. "It's all over now."

But it wasn't over. Kaya thought with alarm, *Magpie! Is Magpie going to be my nickname? Will they never let me forget this?*

24

"These fish need to be prepared," Kaya's grand-mother said to her. "Hold these sticks and give them to me as I need them."

It was later that day, and Aalah was preparing a welcome meal for Kaya's family. She knelt on a tule mat with several salmon in front of her. She was ready to cut up the salmon and place wooden skewers in the pieces so that they could be set by the fire to roast. Other women had dug deep pits to bake camas bulbs in. The delicious scent of roasting food filled the air.

Kaya was glad to be at her grandmother's side. Her head still buzzed with all the trouble she'd caused. Her problems had started with her beloved horse.

"I raced Steps High, but she tried to buck me off," Kaya confessed.

"Hmmm," Aalah muttered. She slid her knife up the belly of a salmon, cut off its head, took out its innards, and began to cut the rest into three long pieces. Her face shone with sweat from the heat of the fires. Her hands glistened with oil from the rich salmon.

25

One by one Kaya handed skewers to Aalah. "But I'm going to train her," Kaya said, thinking out loud. "Someday I'm going to be the very best horsewoman!" When she heard herself boast again, she bit her lip.

"Hmmm," Aalah muttered again. She laced a skewer through a large piece of fish. "I've lived a long time, and I've known many fine horsewomen. First they cared for their families. Then they trained their horses. You must think of others before yourself." She held out her hand for another skewer.

Kaya bowed her head at her grandmother's lecture. She felt a tear run down her nose.

"What's wrong?" Aalah asked. She laid aside a piece of fish and reached for the next one.

"Some children are calling me Magpie. They say I'm no more trustworthy than a thieving bird," Kaya said miserably.

"Nicknames!" Aalah said. "Have I ever told you the awful nickname I got when I was your age?" Her hands never stopped moving as she spoke.

Kaya shook her head. She couldn't imagine her grandmother doing anything to earn an awful nickname.

"Finger Cakes, that's what I was called," Aalah said. "Finger Cakes!"

Kaya couldn't help but smile. Women ground up kouse roots and shaped the mixture into loaves, or little finger cakes, to dry. Everyone liked dried kouse cakes. "That's a funny nickname," Kaya said. "Why did they call you that?"

finger cake

Her grandmother picked up another large salmon. "My mother used to put a few finger cakes into my big brother's shoulder bag," she said. "If he got hungry when he was hunting, he'd chew on the finger cakes. I was jealous that he got extra pieces of my favorite food, so sometimes, when he wasn't looking, I'd steal some of his finger cakes. One day he caught me with my hand in his bag. From then on I was called Finger Cakes."

"Did they call you that for a long time?" Kaya asked.

"Yes, I was Finger Cakes for a long time," Aalah said. "Every time I heard that nickname, I remembered I'd been wrong to steal my brother's food. Every time I heard that nickname, I vowed I'd never again take what wasn't mine. It was a strict teacher, that nickname!"

"But you lost the nickname, didn't you?" Kaya said.

Her grandmother smiled. "Let me tell you something. Sometimes an old friend will call me Finger Cakes just to tease me. After all these years that name still pricks me like a thorn!" She put down her knife and wiped her hands on the grass. "These salmon are ready to roast now."

Kaya was still troubled. "Do you think I can lose my nickname, Aalah?" she asked.

Her grandmother looked closely at Kaya. Her dark eyes seemed to see right into Kaya's heart. "Listen to me," Aalah said. "You're not a little girl any longer. You're growing up. Soon you'll prepare to go on your vision quest to seek your *wyakin*. Work hard to learn your lessons so your nickname won't trouble you. Then your thoughts will be clear when the time comes for your vision quest." She pushed herself up from her knees. "These fish need to be carried to the fire. Everyone is hungry."

◈

Kaya's family gathered beside their tepee for their evening meal. Aalah had laid several tule mats

28

in a row on the grass. The men took their places on one side of the mats. The women set wooden bowls of salmon and baked camas in the center and served the men. Then the women sat down across from them.

Kaya's grandfather led them in giving thanks to *Hun-ya-wat*, the Creator. *Kalutsa* held out his hands over the feast. "Are you paying attention, children?" he asked in his deep voice.

"Aa-heh!" Kaya said with the other children.

"Hun-ya-wat made this earth," Kalutsa said. "He made Nimíipuu and all people. He made all living things on the earth. He made the water and placed the fish in it. He made the sky and placed the birds in it. He created food for all His creatures. We respect and give thanks for His creations." After they all sang a blessing, each one took a sip of water, which sustains all life. Then they all took a tiny bite of salmon, grateful that the fish had given themselves to Nimíipuu for food. After that, Kalutsa motioned for the rest of the food to be passed.

As Kaya ate, she glanced from time to time at the others. She was surrounded by her grandparents, parents, aunts and uncles, and all the children in her family. She gazed at her father with his sharp cheekbones and broad shoulders. She looked at her mother with her shining black hair and her straight brows. Kaya felt how much she loved them all and how much she needed them. She wanted to be worthy of their trust, to be a girl no one would call Magpie ever again.

"It is morning! We are alive! The sun is witness to what we do today!" the camp crier called. He made his way among the tepees to waken everyone and announce the events of that day.

Kaya opened her eyes. Eetsa was already awake. She'd brought a horn bowl of fresh water from the river. Aalah was awake, too. She stood in the doorway of the tepee and faced the east, where the dawn sky glowed pink. With her eyes closed and her chin lifted, Aalah sang a prayer of thanksgiving to Hun-ya-wat, thanking Him for a good night's sleep and the new day. Kaya silently joined Aalah's prayer. Morning prayer songs were rising from all the tepees in the camp.

The prayers over, Kaya stretched and yawned.

Beside her, Speaking Rain rolled onto her back and reached for her folded dress. The twins were sitting on the deerskin blanket they shared. They held out their hands for the root cakes Brown Deer offered them. Brown Deer had arisen before the camp crier passed by, too. Although Kaya hoped to be as hardworking and generous as her older sister, right now Kaya wanted to stay curled up under her soft deerskin as long as possible.

Aalah turned with a smile as if she guessed Kaya's thought. "Come, girls, get up!" she said. "Roll up your bedding. It's time to bathe in the river."

Every single morning of the year, in cold weather as well as warm, all the children went into the river to bathe. The cold water made them strong and healthy. Grandmothers and Whipwoman watched the girls to make sure they got clean.

This morning Kaya delighted in wading into the quiet place at the river bend. A salmon tickled her toes as she walked out on the pebbly bottom to where the water reached her chest. As she splashed, the sun rose over Mount Syringa and flooded light into the green valley.

Rabbit, a girl older than Kaya, ducked

underwater and came up next to her. She shook
drops from her gleaming hair and gave Kaya a sly
smile. "I didn't know magpies could swim," she
whispered.

Kaya's cheeks burned. "I can swim, and faster
than you!" she said.

"Will you peck if you catch me?" Rabbit laughed.
With strong strokes she began to swim for shore.

Kaya swam after her. She could almost touch
Rabbit's flashing heels, but she couldn't catch up to
her. Kaya waded out of the river with her head bent.
"Magpie didn't win that race," Rabbit said with a grin.

That nickname stung like a hornet. *I let myself
boast again!* Kaya realized with dismay as she dressed.

Kaya returned to their tepee, where she found
her parents talking and laughing quietly together as
Eetsa braided Toe-ta's thick black hair. When Eetsa
had tied his braids together, Toe-ta beckoned to
Kaya. "Let's go work with your horse," he said.

Toe-ta kept his best stallion, Runner, tethered on
a long rope near the camp. He put a horsehair rope
on Runner's lower jaw and mounted him bareback.
He handed Kaya another rope bit and a long rope to
carry. Then he lifted her up behind him on the big

32

horse, and they set out toward the herd.

Kaya loved to ride with her father. She leaned against his warm back. The smooth gait of Toe-ta's stallion rocked them gently. "Toe-ta, Steps High tried to buck me off yesterday," she said.

"I thought so," Toe-ta said. "I saw you walking her. If you hadn't had trouble, you'd have been riding."

"I know your horse would never buck you," Kaya said.

Toe-ta was quiet for a little while. "Have I told you about the first time my father put me on a horse?" he said.

"You've never told me that," Kaya said.

"I was a little boy, even younger than your brothers," Toe-ta said. "One day my father put me on the gentle old horse my grandmother rode. He told me to ride around the camp slowly. But after I went around slowly, I wanted to go faster. I kicked the horse as I'd seen my grandmother do. The horse bolted! My father chased us, yelling to me to turn the horse uphill to slow him. I looked for a soft spot and jumped off into the grass instead."

"Were you hurt, Toe-ta?" Kaya asked.

"I was sore all over!" he said. "Do you know

why I told you that story today?"

"Why, Toe-ta?" Kaya asked.

"I want you to know that no one is born know-ing how to ride," he said. "And you have to respect the horse you're riding. It takes a lot of work to learn what we need to know in this life."

Toe-ta swung Runner alongside a group of mares. Steps High was grazing with them.

"Whistle for your horse," he told Kaya. "She knows your whistle."

When Steps High heard Kaya's whistle, she pricked up her ears. As she came forward, Toe-ta tossed a rope around her neck and drew her close.

Each time Kaya saw Steps High, she marveled at her horse's beauty. Steps High was both graceful and strong, the muscles rippling under her skin.

Toe-ta got off his stallion and lifted Kaya down. As he approached Steps High, she tossed her small head and rolled her eyes. Toe-ta put the rope bit in her mouth, then grabbed a handful of mane as he swung onto her back. He held the rope reins firmly as he rode her away from the herd at a trot. Steps High pranced nervously, but she obeyed Toe-ta.

He drew the horse to a halt again by Kaya. "Now it's your turn," he said. "You're a strong rider. If you need me, I'm here to help."

Kaya swung up onto her horse. Toe-ta handed her the reins. But Kaya didn't urge Steps High forward.

"I won't push you too fast or too hard again," she whispered to her horse. "I want you to trust me."

Kaya pressed her knees to her horse's sides. She could feel a shiver run down her horse's back as Steps High began to walk. Steps High pushed against the bit as if she were thinking about running and bucking again, but she stayed at a walk until

Kaya nudged her to trot. Kaya kept her horse gathered in and rode in slow circles until Toe-ta motioned for her to come back to him.

He took her horse's reins in one hand and stroked Steps High's neck. "Tawts," he said to Kaya. "That's just how you must ride her for a long time. Stay slow and stay in control. Work with her a little longer, then come back to camp." Toe-ta turned Runner and rode off.

As Kaya rode her horse in another circle, Fox Tail rode up beside her. He'd been helping some older boys with the horses. His face was dusty and his lips were dry. Herding was hard work in the hot sun. "Do you want to race again?" he asked Kaya.

"Toe-ta said I can't race my horse for a long time," Kaya said.

Fox Tail's grin was a wicked one. "I forgot that magpies don't race!" he cried. He kicked his horse and galloped away from her.

That nickname again! It gave Kaya a sick feeling in her stomach. She clenched her teeth as she circled Steps High back to the herd.

CHAPTER
THREE
—

COURTSHIP DANCE

One morning, after many days of clear skies, dark clouds rolled over the mountains and rain pelted down. The tule reeds of the tepee coverings swelled with water and kept out the rain. The women turned from preparing food to work they could do inside the dry, cozy tepees until the storm passed.

Aalah took out the hemp cord and the bear grass she needed to weave some flat bags. She'd dyed the bear grass soft shades of red, green, and yellow. She gave some brown cord to Kaya, then started a bag for Speaking Rain to work on. Although Speaking Rain couldn't see, she could make fine cord and could weave by touch once Aalah set the first rows.

Eetsa and Brown Deer were mending moccasins for the twins, who napped on their deerskins. As he always did, Wing Feather slept with his hand tucked into his baby moccasin, which he cradled under his chin.

For a long time they worked in silence. Kaya liked the quiet tepee. The sound of rain falling on the tule mats soothed her. In fact, she wished she could stay inside their tepee, where no one called her Magpie, and never go out again.

Aalah touched Kaya's weaving to show her where her work was lumpy and uneven. "You're awake, but you're dreaming," Aalah said. "Will you tell me your dream?"

Kaya undid the line of weaving and started it over. She didn't want to admit how much that nickname still troubled her. "I was dreaming about my horse," she said.

"When I was a girl we didn't dream of horses," Aalah said with a smile. "When I was a girl we didn't even have horses. When we traveled we walked on our own two feet, and our strong dogs pulled our loads for us."

"You know about these things," Eetsa said

respectfully. "But dogs couldn't pull the big loads that our horses do. And we couldn't travel as fast on foot as we can on horseback."

"But our scouts could run fast!" Aalah said. "The scouts who lived near the trail to enemy country ran as fast as the wind to warn us of danger." Aalah's fingers flew as she wove the bag. Already she'd finished a plain border and was adding a lovely pattern of triangles.

"It's true the scouts were swift," Eetsa said. "But no man runs as fast as a horse. No man can travel as far on foot as he can on horseback." She began sewing a new sole onto a moccasin with a length of sinew.

"Now the men ride far away, but often they don't come back for a long, long time," Aalah said. "Things were better in the old days."

"I can't imagine our warriors without their horses," Brown Deer said softly. "A warrior is so fierce on horseback! He fights so bravely!"

"Our men were brave warriors long before they ever heard of horses," Aalah said. "And because we have horses, our enemies make more raids on us."

"Aa-heh," Eetsa said. "You're right. But without

his horse my husband wouldn't be such a good hunter. He couldn't bring us so much meat. He always gives meat to the old people, too."

"Horses are so beautiful!" Kaya chimed in. "Especially the spotted ones, like Steps High!" She imagined her horse running with her head held high and her black tail streaming. Was it boasting to call her beautiful?

Aalah reached for Kaya's bag and gently took it from her. When Aalah put the tip of her finger through a hole in a loose row, Kaya realized that she hadn't made the weaving tight enough. She began to unravel her work so that she could make it better.

"Aalah, you've often said we need horses for many things," Brown Deer said.

Aalah sighed deeply. "I've said so and it's true," she said. "The old days are gone. We can't unravel our lives and begin them again, as Kaya is doing with her weaving." She put down her work and placed her hands on her knees. "I want you to listen to me. I'm going to tell you something."

Kaya and Speaking Rain laid down their weaving at once. Eetsa and Brown Deer stopped sewing. When Aalah spoke like that, she wanted their attention.

"I've lived a long time, and I remember many things," Aalah said. "Isn't that so?"

Eetsa and Brown Deer nodded.

"Aa-heh," Kaya and Speaking Rain said.

"One thing I remember is the time of terrible sickness," Aalah said. "Traders told us about strangers with pale, hairy faces who rode from far away to trade at the Big River. With the strangers on horses came a sickness of fevers and blisters, a sickness we'd never known before. My people never saw the strangers with pale faces, but their sickness came to us anyway. Many, many people sickened and died. The most powerful medicine man had no medicine to cure this new sickness."

Aalah was quiet for a while, gazing into space. Then she ran her hands across her cheeks. "You see these pockmarks on my face," she said. "I was one who got the sickness. My own mother died of it— I've told you that, too. These pockmarks remind me how few of us survived. They remind me that not just good things came into our lives with the horses. But the marks also remind me to be strong and help others."

Kaya looked at Aalah's solemn face. She knew

*"With the strangers on horses came a sickness of fevers and blisters,
a sickness we'd never known before," Aalah said.*

Aalah was thinking about the bad times in the past. Kaya was ashamed to be worrying about an unpleasant nickname when so much suffering had come to others. Would difficult times like the sickness come again to Nimíipuu?

"We've talked enough of that," Aalah said. "It's time to go back to work."

Kaya began her weaving again, making each twist of cord as firm and as tight as possible. When she grew up, she wanted to be a wise, strong woman like Aalah.

⚜

"The men are getting out the drums again!" Speaking Rain said. "Soon they'll start singing. Listen!"

Kaya listened. From across the camp came the first drumbeats. Every evening, drumming, songs, and laughter filled the air. In the middle of the camp, Toe-ta and some other men were playing the stick game, joking and shouting as they made their guesses. The women watched and chatted with their friends. The children chased each other and played games. Soon there would be dancing, too, until it

was time for the men to light fires along the riverbank and begin their night fishing. Kaya loved being
part of so much excitement.

In their tepee, Kaya watched Brown Deer
dressing herself for the courtship dance. Brown Deer
put on her best dress, decorated with porcupine
quills and elk teeth. She tied on her wide belt and
hung a small woven bag from it. She smoothed the
ankle flaps of her moccasins and tied them neatly.

"Your dress is so beautiful!" Kaya exclaimed.

Speaking Rain folded her arms and grinned up
at her older sister. "Tell us, who do you want to
dance with tonight?"

"I don't know," Brown Deer said with a shrug
and the flicker of a smile.

As Brown Deer hurried to join the others, Kaya
thought her big sister was the prettiest girl in the
whole village.

Kaya and Speaking Rain followed her out of
the tepee. In the light of the rising moon, the twins
were dancing, hopping about and bobbing their
heads like quail. Wing Feather beat two sticks
together. Sparrow turned around and around until
he was dizzy and fell to his knees.

Kaya was too young to join the courtship dance, but the drumbeats and singing made her want to whirl around and around like Sparrow. They made her want to beat the rhythm like Wing Feather. As Kaya listened, she practiced dancing by taking small steps, moving in place. Who could resist the drums!

On one side of the clearing, the older girls began to form a circle. The older boys formed a circle around the girls for the courtship dance. In this dance a boy tried to dance beside the girl he liked best. If a girl let him stay by her side, that meant she liked him best, too. Most families decided who would marry whom, but some paid attention to the choices of the dancers in the courtship dance.

"Brown Deer's dancing near us," Kaya whispered to Speaking Rain.

"Is she looking at any special boy?" Speaking Rain asked.

"She looks at all the boys but one," Kaya said. "She never looks at Cut Cheek."

Cut Cheek was slim and strong. He was a good hunter and a good dancer, too. The scar on his cheek only made him better-looking, Kaya thought. She'd often seen him glance at Brown Deer as he danced,

45

but Brown Deer never returned his gaze.

"When Cut Cheek comes near, Brown Deer looks at her moccasins," Kaya said. "I don't think she likes him at all."

Speaking Rain giggled. "Kaya, you're foolish!" she said. "If Brown Deer can't bring herself to look at Cut Cheek, that means she really likes him."

"But how will he know she likes him if she never looks at him?" Kaya wondered.

"He'll know!" Speaking Rain said.

All the young men and women were in the circle now. When the drumbeats changed, the boys and girls danced slowly forward toward each other. The long fringes on the girls' dresses rippled and swung as the girls moved. The drums seemed to be saying, *Come dance with me! Dance with me!* With exciting music like this, how could the dancers keep their steps so steady and even?

"Where's Cut Cheek dancing?" Speaking Rain asked.

"He's on the other side of the circle," Kaya said. "I don't think he'll be able to get near Brown Deer."

The dancers moved close to each other, then

away, then close again. The next time they were close, a boy eased himself out of his line and placed a stick on a girl's right shoulder. She kept the stick on her shoulder and made room for him by her side. Now they danced as a couple.

The dancers moved toward each other again. As they advanced, Cut Cheek managed to move past the boy next to him. Now he was almost in front of Brown Deer. She held her chin high and looked straight ahead. She made the fringe on her dress snap with each graceful step.

"What's happening now?" Speaking Rain demanded.

"Cut Cheek keeps moving closer to Brown Deer," Kaya said.

Again the dancers moved forward. The boy called Jumps Back moved opposite Brown Deer. He was short, with broad shoulders. Although he often liked to tease the girls, now he looked very serious. When Brown Deer danced close to him, Jumps Back stepped beside her and placed his stick on her shoulder. With a shrug, she knocked the stick off. Jumps Back bent to pick up his stick, and Cut Cheek moved into his place. Now he was opposite Brown Deer.

"Brown Deer just turned down Jumps Back," Kaya told Speaking Rain. "Cut Cheek is right in front of her. But she's looking past him as if she doesn't even know he's there."

"Oh, she knows he's there!" Speaking Rain giggled.

The next time the dancers were close, Cut Cheek left the boys' line. His dark face was gleaming. He stepped next to Brown Deer and placed his stick on her shoulder. Blushing, she took a deep breath as if she were about to dive into deep water. She let his stick stay on her shoulder, and they danced now side by side.

"She chose Cut Cheek!" Kaya said. "She didn't hesitate for a moment!"

⁂

The run of salmon up the river was coming to an end. Many, many salmon had given themselves to Nimíipuu. The women had packed the dried salmon into large, woven bags and parfleches made of rawhide. Now they were packing up their belongings as well. Soon the women would roll up the tule mat coverings of the tepees and take down the tepee poles. They would put everything they owned on their horses and the travois and set out. It was time to move higher into the mountains so that the women could pick huckleberries and the men could hunt for elk and deer. Kaya and her family would

parfleche

be part of the group traveling back to Salmon River Country.

Aalah called Kaya to her. She looked worried. "I think I left my knife where we were working yesterday," Aalah said.

"I'll go look carefully," Kaya said.

Kaya already had a rope bit on Steps High. She'd been riding her horse every day, keeping her tightly reined in and held to a trot. Steps High hadn't once tried to buck off Kaya. But Kaya hadn't yet asked Toe-ta if it was safe to run her horse again.

"May I come with you, Kaya?" Speaking Rain asked. Kaya gave Speaking Rain her hand and pulled her sister up onto the horse to sit behind her. Riding bareback, they trotted away from the camp.

At the river, they passed Toe-ta and a few other men fishing for the last of the salmon. As the men speared fish, Fox Tail

49

and some other boys put the salmon into baskets.

Toe-ta stood on the bank with his back to the sun. He had placed a large white stone in the current where the river was shallow. When a fish swam between the white stone and Toe-ta, he could see its outline and spear it.

Downstream, where the river was deeper, Aalah had been cleaning fish on the bank the day before. Kaya reined in Steps High. "I'll start searching a little way down the path and make my way back to you," Kaya told Speaking Rain. "Wait here to mark where I started my search." Speaking Rain slipped off Steps High. As Kaya rode on down the path, she looked for her grandmother's knife.

Steps High was tense and skittish. She shied at a garter snake crossing the path, but Kaya steadied her. When Steps High shied a second time, Kaya reined her in. "What's the matter, girl?" Kaya asked. "What's spooking you?" Steps High snorted and pawed the ground.

Kaya shaded her eyes and looked back to where Speaking Rain had been waiting. Speaking Rain was cautiously making her way through the elderberry

bushes that grew along the riverbank. She couldn't know there was a steep bank on the other side of the bushes. "Stop, Speaking Rain!" Kaya called. She turned Steps High and started back.

Speaking Rain didn't seem to hear Kaya's call. Were Stick People leading her astray? She kept going. "Stop! Don't take another step!" Kaya cried.

Now Speaking Rain heard Kaya's cry. She stopped and turned. As she did, a piece of the bank crumbled beneath her feet. Speaking Rain fell backward. In a shower of stones, she tumbled into the swift river!

CHAPTER
FOUR
—

RESCUED FROM
THE RIVER

Kaya drove Steps High forward. She
jumped her over the bushes and reined
her in sharply, her hooves plowing
the ground. Speaking Rain was struggling in deep
water, trying to swim toward shore. As she thrashed,
a branch plunged down in the swift current and hit
her. She went under. When she came up again, she
was being pulled downstream in the powerful surge
of the river.

Fear struck through Kaya like a lightning flash.
If Speaking Rain wasn't pulled from the river, she'd
drown. If Kaya tried to swim after her, they could
both drown. To save Speaking Rain, Kaya's only
hope was to run her horse along the bank, try to get

ahead of Speaking Rain, and ride into the river to catch her.

Kaya gave her horse her head, then kicked her. Steps High burst forward. In a few strides she was at a full gallop. Kaya leaned low over her neck, clasping her horse with her knees. What if another piece of riverbank gave way? What if her horse bucked? Steps High lengthened out and tore around the next bend, then the next. She seemed as swift as a hawk diving from the sky! Now they were ahead of Speaking Rain, who flailed in the churning river. From here, Kaya had to get her horse into the water and then swim upstream to meet Speaking Rain as she was swept down.

Would Steps High obey Kaya's command to swim? Kaya dug her heels into her horse's sides and again urged her forward. Steps High crossed the beach but paused at the edge of the water. "Come on, girl!" Kaya said, giving her another kick. Then Kaya felt Steps High become one with her again. The horse moved out into the icy current until she was swimming.

Kaya angled her horse upstream. She held tightly to Steps High's mane to keep her balance

against the swirling currents. She'd have to catch
Speaking Rain as soon as she came within reach,
or else Speaking Rain would be swept under the
horse's sharp hooves. In another moment, Speaking
Rain was upon her. Kaya reached and grasped,
caught her arm—she had her! She pulled and
dragged Speaking Rain over her horse's withers.
Holding Speaking Rain tightly, Kaya turned her
horse downstream. She felt Steps High gather
herself.

The horse's strokes evened out as she calmed.
But Speaking Rain was limp against Kaya. Was she
breathing? Kaya headed Steps High toward shore.

In a few more strokes, her horse's hooves
touched bottom. Steps High's head came up, and
she climbed onto the sandy beach. She shook her
head and pranced a step or two as if she knew
she'd done something to be proud of.

Kaya slid off her horse and caught Speaking
Rain as her sister slipped down into her arms.
Speaking Rain lifted her head, moaned, and began
to cough up water. "You're safe, Speaking Rain!"
Kaya said against her drenched head. "You're safe!"

Toe-ta appeared on the bank above them. He

In another moment, Speaking Rain was upon her. Kaya reached and grasped, caught her arm—she had her!

was followed by the other fishermen and by Fox
Tail. Toe-ta leaped down onto the sand. He took
Speaking Rain into his arms, bent her forward, and
slapped her back with his cupped hand to force
more water from her.

Kaya's teeth were chattering. "Speaking Rain,
can you get your breath?" she asked.

"Aa-heh," Speaking Rain gasped.

"I heard you shout and I ran," Toe-ta said. "I saw
what happened. You did well, Kaya. Your horse did
well, too."

"Steps High knew Speaking Rain needed us,"
Kaya said. "She did everything I asked of her."

"She did what you asked because she trusts
you," Toe-ta said. "You've earned her trust,
remember that."

Fox Tail crouched on the bank. Was that a look
of admiration in his eyes? "You told me you couldn't
race," he said. "But you were racing like wildfire,
Kaya."

"Kaya wasn't racing to be the fastest," Toe-ta
corrected him. "She was racing to save Speaking
Rain's life."

Toe-ta's words lifted Kaya's heart. He knew she

hadn't acted for herself, but for Speaking Rain. And Fox Tail had called her Kaya, not Magpie!

Kaya closed her eyes, pressed her face against Steps High's warm, wet neck, and felt the powerful pulse beating there. "*Katsee-yow-yow*, my horse!" she whispered gratefully. Then she held the bridle so that Toe-ta could lift Speaking Rain onto Steps High's back and they could take her back to camp.

The horses needed fresh grass before they could begin the journey higher into the mountains. Kaya rode with Raven, Fox Tail, and some older boys and girls to herd the horses to new pasture. As Kaya rode, she gazed up at a tall peak. She knew the story of how the mountain came to be. An old chief had a vision. His vision told him that men with pale faces would come to steal the shining rocks scattered here. To protect their shining rocks, the people gathered them into a pile and built the mountain over them to hide them. Their treasure was saved because of the old chief's vision.

Kaya thought that if she'd lived in those days, she'd have helped build the mountain over the shining rocks. After all, her name—*Kaya'aton'my'*—meant "she who arranges rocks." Her mother gave her that name because the first thing she saw after Kaya's birth was a woman arranging rocks to heat a sweat lodge.

Will one of us be given a vision someday? Kaya wondered. *Will I?*

She knew that one day soon, like all the other boys and girls, she would go on her vision quest. *Will I be ready when that time comes?* she thought.

When she went into the mountains on her quest, Kaya would seek her wyakin. If her wyakin came to her, she could also receive special powers. Would the hawk give her the ability to see far? Would the canyon wren give her the power to defend her family, the way the wren drives off rattlesnakes? *What creature will my wyakin be?* Kaya wondered. She hoped it would give her powers and a vision to help Nimíipuu, like the old chief in the story.

Fox Tail rode past, his big roan kicking up a cloud of dust. *Fox Tail's too much of a rascal to become a leader of our people,* Kaya thought. But maybe the old chief, whose vision saved the shining mountain, had once been a bothersome boy like Fox Tail.

Kaya reminded herself to think of the work
of the day and to do her job well. A frisky young
stallion bolted out of the herd and passed behind
Kaya and her horse. Immediately, she swung
Steps High around, dug in her heels, and galloped
after the runaway. Steps High knew her job, too. In a
burst of speed, she caught up to the frisky horse and
drove him back into the herd again. "Tawts!" Kaya
said, and patted Steps High's shoulder. "Tawts, my
beautiful horse!"

Looking
Back
1764

A PEEK INTO
THE PAST

For countless generations, grandparents have told children like Kaya stories
for fun and for education. Through stories
about a character named Coyote as well as
other animals, Nimíipuu children learned
about the world around them, how to behave
and how not to behave, and the traditions and
history of their people. Elders told children the
following story to explain how Nimíipuu believe
they—and other people—came to be.

According to legend, long before there were
any humans on the earth, the animals could talk,
and they acted like people. One day, a greedy monster
came along and started eating everything in its path.

Coyote is an important character
in hundreds of legends.

After a while, Coyote decided the time had come to stop the monster. He hid a bone knife in his mouth and tricked the monster into swallowing him. Once inside, he built a huge fire in the monster's stomach. Then he used his knife to cut out the monster's heart. The monster died, and all the animals he had swallowed escaped. Coyote cut the monster into pieces and flung them to the four winds. Wherever a piece landed, a group of humans was born. Each group had its own strengths and characteristics. After all the pieces of the monster had been scattered, Fox pointed out that Coyote had not put any humans in the beautiful spot where he and Coyote were standing. So Coyote sprinkled some blood from the monster's heart onto the ground.

Near Kamiah, Idaho, you can visit the Heart of the Monster landmark.

From the monster's lifeblood sprang the last group of humans—Nimíipuu, which means "The People."

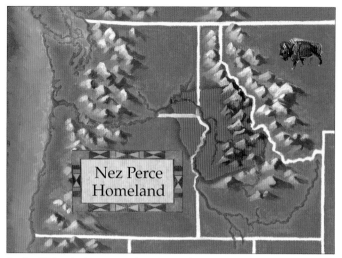

In the 1750s, the Nez Perces' territory, shown on the map in red, covered about 27,000 square miles of modern-day Idaho, Washington, and Oregon.

Today, Nimíipuu are known as the *Nez Perce*, which is French for "pierced nose." Early white explorers, including French fur trappers, mistakenly believed that all Nez Perce wore shells through their noses and gave them that name.

In Kaya's time, Nez Perce people lived in the forested mountains, grassy hills and prairies, and steep canyons of present-day Idaho, Washington, and Oregon. They visited, married, and occasionally fought with their many neighbors, including Coeur d'Alenes and Spokanes to the northeast, Palouses, Umatillas, Yakamas, and Cayuses to the west and northwest, and Shoshones to the south.

Salmon and other fish made up a large part of the Nez Perces' diet. Some salmon were as big as a small child!

Nez Perces traveled with the seasons throughout this vast territory to gather food and to hunt and fish. They traveled outside of their homeland as well. In the spring and summer, they sometimes went all the way west to the Columbia River Gorge to fish and trade or east into the Great Plains to hunt buffalo.

While traveling, Nez Perces set up temporary camps of small tepees covered with lightweight mats woven from tule (TOO-lee) reeds. Then, every fall, the people settled back into their permanent winter villages in warm valleys along rivers and streams.

The main winter village building was a longhouse covered with tule mats. Longhouses could be more than 100 feet long and house more than 20 families. Several extended families—parents, grandparents, aunts, uncles, cousins— lived together in each longhouse.

Nez Perce children spent much of their time with grandparents and with siblings and cousins, all of whom they thought of as brothers and sisters.

Women gathered tule reeds, which they dried and then wove into mats to cover their lodgings.

Boys and girls were taught to behave respectfully and responsibly. But when one child disobeyed or misbehaved, the entire group might be switched by an elder called the Whipman or Whipwoman. The children learned, as Kaya did, that what one person does affects the safety and well-being of everyone.

Nez Perces called their Creator Hun-ya-wat. They believed that everything He created—the earth, the sky, the seas and rivers, and all the creatures in nature—had spirits and special powers. Guardian spirits, called wyakins, gave these special powers to humans through visions and helped them throughout their lives.

Some Nez Perces also had visions that their way of life would one day change. And they were right. The first sign of change was the horse. Spanish explorers brought horses to the Americas in the 1500s. Two hundred years later, the Nez Perces traded for their first horses, perhaps with the Shoshone Indians to the south. Nez Perces quickly became excellent horsemen and horsewomen. They

Small groups of women rode for days to gather food for their families and village. Horses made this important job faster and easier.

knew how to breed the animals to produce stronger and swifter horses.

Nez Perces could travel farther and faster on horse-back. As they met and traded with new people, they learned new ways of

Among the Nez Perces' herds were spotted horses, which are known today as Appaloosas.

doing things. Goods such as beads and blankets from Europe began to trickle to the Nez Perces before they ever saw a white person. And so did something deadlier. Diseases brought to America by whites wiped out entire Indian villages. Thousands of Indians, like Kaya's grand-mother, Aalah, sickened from diseases like smallpox, and many died.

Most Nez Perces saw their first white people in the fall of 1805, when Kaya would have been 50 years old. That's when the men of the Lewis and Clark Expedition stumbled out of the Bitterroot Mountains and into a Nez Perce camp. The explorers were starving and freezing, and the Nez Perces befriended them, took care of them, and helped them resume their journey. In later years, white missionaries and settlers came to Nez Perce country and were treated kindly, too.

Despite the friendliness Nez Perces showed to whites, the United States government took away most of the Nez Perces' homeland in the mid-1800s so that white pioneers could settle on it. The government set aside a small tract of land in Idaho for all Nez Perce people to live on, called the Nez Perce Reservation.

> *". . decended the mountain to a leavel pine Countrey proceeded on through a butifull Countrey for three miles to a Small Plain in which I found maney Indian lodges, at the distance of 1 mile from the lodges I met 3 Indian boys, when they Saw me [they] ran and hid themselves in the grass . . ."*
> —Clark, September 20, 1805

The U.S. government tried to force Indians on reservations to *assimilate*—to give up their traditional ways and live like white people. Children were put into missionary schools to learn English and were punished if they spoke their own language. The reservation land was divided up into small parcels and given to individual Indians, instead of being shared by all. The government expected Indians to make a living by farming instead of hunting and gathering their food.

Today, Nez Perce Indians still live on reservations in Idaho, Washington, Oregon, and Canada, and in other places within their traditional homeland.

Original Nez Perce homeland

Present Nez Perce Reservation

Confederated Tribes of the Umatilla Indian Reservation

Confederated Tribes of the Colville Reservation

Peigan Indian Reserve

On reservations in the mid-1800s, Nez Perces began to give up their buckskin clothing and wear cotton and wool, just like white people.

Others live throughout the country and around the world. Nez Perce children, like children everywhere, attend school, participate in sports, and play computer games. But many also learn the Nez Perce language, dance in pow-wows, and play traditional Indian games.

The Nez Perce people look back on their history with pride, and they look toward their future with confidence.

Nez Perce children today embrace both cultures—modern and traditional.

Glossary of Nez Perce Words

In the story, Nez Perce words are spelled so that English readers can pronounce them. Here, you can also see how the words are actually spelled and said by the Nez Perce people.

Phonetic/Nez Perce	Pronunciation	Meaning
aa-heh/ʼéehe	*AA-heh*	yes, that's right
Aalah/Eelé	*AA-lah*	grandmother from father's side
Eetsa/Iice	*EET-sah*	Mother
Hun-ya-wat/ Hanyawʼáat	*hun-yah-WAHT*	the Creator
Kalutsa/ Qalacá	*kah-luht-SAH*	grandfather from father's side
katsee-yow-yow/ qeʼciʼyewʼyew'	*KAHT-see-yow-yow*	thank you
Kayaʼatonʼmy'	*ky-YAAH-a-ton-my*	she who arranges rocks
Nimíipuu	*Nee-MEE-poo*	The People; known today as the Nez Perce Indians
tawts/taʼc	*TAWTS*	good
tawts may-we/ taʼc méeywi	*TAWTS MAY-wee*	good morning
Toe-ta/Tootʼa	*TOH-tah*	Father
Wallowa/ Walʼáwa	*wah-LAU-wa*	Wallowa Valley in present-day Oregon
wyakin/ wéeyekin	*WHY-ah-kin*	guardian spirit